Ruth Symes thinks the next best thing to being magic is writing stories about magic. She lives in Bedfordshire and when she isn't writing she can be found by the river walking her dog, Traffy (who is often in the river).

Find out more on her website: www.ruthsymes.com.

Marion Lindsay has always loved stories and pictures, so it made perfect sense when she decided to become a children's book illustrator and won the Egmont Best New Talent Award. She lives and works in Cambridge and in her spare time paints glass and makes jewelry.

Find out more at: www.marionlindsay.co.uk.

Ruth Symes

Bella Donna

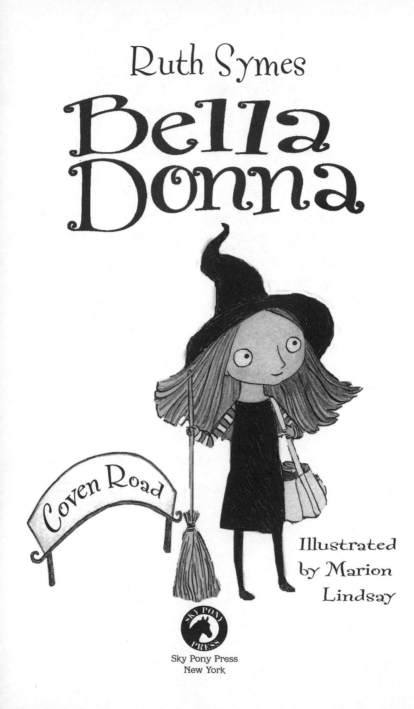

Coven Road

Illustrated
by Marion
Lindsay

SKY PONY
PRESS

Sky Pony Press
New York

Chapter 1

I wanted to be a witch from the day I was born. Or at least I think I did. Of course, I can't remember actually being born. I can't even remember being left on the doorstep of Templeton Children's Home when I was a baby—although I can remember farther back than anyone else I know.

My first real memory is lying in my crib and looking up at a painted wooden lady with a pointy hat and four broomsticks flying around her. The witch mobile had been left alongside me on that doorstep. It kept me amused for hours. My little hands and feet never tired of stretching up to try to touch it.

It was a wintry night and there was a storm outside. I was awake, just looking at my witch mobile dancing in the moonlight. Sam, the baby in the next crib, started to snore—babies snore an awful lot and make snuffly blocked-up-nose noises. I looked at the pacifier stuffed in his mouth. Every now and again he'd suck contentedly on it. As I looked at Sam with the pacifier in his mouth I wanted that pacifier. Oh how I wanted it! I wanted it more than I'd wanted anything before.

I don't know how or what exactly happened, but one moment I wanted the pacifier really, *really* badly and the next moment I had it! And I was sucking on it as hard as I could. Even with Sam's dribble all over it, it was lovely. It took my mind off hunger; it took my mind off everything. It made me start to feel happy and sleepy.

Of course Sam wasn't exactly pleased to have lost the pacifier and he started screaming. He wouldn't shut up for a long time—he was trying to tell Nurse Harrigan that his precious pacifier had been stolen, but she didn't understand.

I continued sucking happily and looked at my witch mobile. The witch danced about in the moonlight and seemed to smile at me.

You'd have thought all the babies at Templeton Children's Home would have been adopted super fast and lots of them were—but not me. And not Sam either.

By the time we were five, lots of people had wanted to adopt me because I was sweet and cute, and lots of people had wanted to adopt Sam, too—but we didn't want to be adopted by just anybody. We wanted our Forever Families to be perfect and if that meant waiting a little bit longer than everyone else . . . well, then we'd wait. None of the children were ever asked to go and live with someone they didn't want to live with—that wouldn't have been fair.

One day we had a meeting in our den, which was the old greenhouse at the back of the children's home. Sam had found it by accident when he was following a ladybug to see where it lived. You had to go through a lot of stinging nettles and brambles to get to it and it wasn't exactly a place many people would want to visit—so it was perfect for us.

The windows were either broken with plants poking through or were covered with green sludge. Only the hardiest of plants—weeds—survived.

I spat on the palm of my hand and then Sam spat on his palm and we pressed our two palms together and made a pact that we wouldn't settle for second best.

I, of course, wanted a family that didn't mind me wanting to be a witch. Sam wanted a Forever Family who liked worms and bugs, like he did. Sam was always getting covered in mud or soaked in puddles or dirty pond water in his quest to find a toad or a spider or some other creepy crawly thing. Once Nurse Harrigan even found a frog in his pocket—he said he was rescuing it.

Nurse Harrigan had told Sam more than once that he'd have to change his ways if he wanted to be adopted, but Sam didn't listen. He was sure there was a Forever Family out there, somewhere, that would like him just the way he was. And if he liked them too then they'd be the people he'd choose to adopt him.

And I was sure there was a family out there who wouldn't mind me wanting to be a witch. And that would be the family I'd choose to adopt me.

It was just taking them a little while to find us, that was all.

★ ★ ★

Remember Sam's pacifier? Well, a few other strange things happened over the years that I couldn't explain. The first one was just after we'd started nursery school. I loved my nursery school teacher, Miss Willow, and I thought I would like her to adopt me. But then I was painting a picture of a witch one day, and she said she didn't like witches. The moment she'd said that, black paint splattered all down her floaty pink dress. I don't know how it happened. One moment the paint was in the pot and the next moment it had all flown out and landed on Miss Willow. She wasn't pleased and told me I was a very naughty girl. It wasn't my fault though. I hadn't done anything.

Then, when we were six, Sam and I got invited to Angela's fancy dress party. Angela was in the same class as us at school but she didn't really like me or Sam much and she didn't talk to us or want to sit next to us or play with us. I think Angela's mom made a mistake when she was giving out the invitations. No one ever usually invited us to anything. Sam was really excited because he'd heard that Angela had a pond in her garden, with lizards in it. I was really excited because I'd never been to a party outside the children's home before, let alone a party where I could dress up as anyone I liked. We had a dressing-up box at Templeton and inside it was a witch's hat and dress. I knew who I was going to the party as.

When we got to the party Sam ran off to the pond and I found out that I was the only one dressed as a witch. Every other girl was either a fairy or a princess.

"You're It, Bella Donna," Angela said later on, when we were playing hide-and-seek. Everyone ran away and hid while I closed my eyes and counted to a hundred.

"Seven . . . ten . . . twenty-three . . . thirty-six, ninety-two . . ." Close enough—I was only six and not very good at math. But it was very easy to find them. As soon as I opened my eyes all I had to do was concentrate and I just knew where they were—it was like magic.

"Angela's up a tree. Sarah and Jane are behind the trash cans. Tracey's in the toilet!" I shouted from where I was standing.

The other children weren't pleased.

"You cheated!" someone said.

"No, I didn't."

"You must have been looking. There's no way you could see us behind the trash cans."

I hadn't been cheating—I'd just known.

"What would you like in your sandwich, Bella Donna?" Angela's mom asked me when we went inside for the birthday lunch.

"A mouse," I said. "Witches like mouse sandwiches and bug jelly."

"Urgh! Yuck! You're horrible, Bella Donna," the other girls said.

"Your name even sounds like a witch's name," Angela said.

"Good!" I grinned to show my blacked-out front teeth—I'd used Angela's mom's mascara that I'd found when I went to the bathroom. There was also some deep purple eye shadow and black nail polish in the bathroom cupboard that I'd been tempted to try, but I hadn't.

"Most of all I'd like some snot ice cream," I continued. "Lovely and green, yum, yum, yum!"

"I think I'm going to be sick," said Angela.

I laughed my witch's cackle that I'd been practicing especially for the party.

At that moment, Sam came in from the garden dripping with pond water and holding a lizard.

"I found one!" he said.

"Quick—put it in my sandwich," I said. (Although, of course, I wouldn't have eaten a lizard really—I was only joking. But it was fun to see everyone squirm.)

Angela's mom phoned the children's home and Maisie, one of the house parents from Templeton, came to pick us up.

"We're so sorry," Maisie told Angela's mom.

"If I'd known what they were like, I'd never have invited them," she replied.

Maisie looked at me suspiciously. "One minute," she said, and her lightning fingers pulled the eye shadow and nail polish out from under my witch's hat and gave them back to Angela's mom.

"I don't know how they got there," I said, shocked. I really, really didn't know how they'd got under my hat. But neither Maisie nor Angela's mom believed me.

"It's all your fault!" I told Sam on the drive home. "Stupid lizard hunter."

"It's all your fault for wanting to be a stupid witch all the time," Sam shouted back at me.

Maisie took us straight to Nurse Harrigan's office. Nurse Harrigan had been promoted and was now the matron.

Maisie knocked on the door and Nurse Harrigan shouted, "Come in!"

Sam and I stood in front of Nurse Harrigan's desk. She was very, very angry. "You have let down this children's home and I am very disappointed with you both," she said.

Sam and I looked down at our shoes.

"From now on Sam, you may not play with lizards, worms, or any other creatures."

"But they're my friends . . ."

"Do you want to be adopted?"

"Yes, Nurse Harrigan," Sam said. "But —" I knew he was about to tell her he only wanted to be adopted by a family that liked him playing with lizards and worms and other creatures.

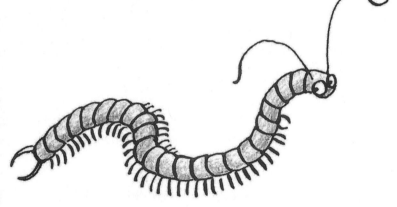

"Then you'll do what I say," she interrupted.

"Yes, Nurse Harrigan," Sam said. I saw him cross his fingers behind his back, so I knew he didn't mean it.

"And as for you, Isabella . . ."

I wanted to remind her that I like to be called

Bella Donna, but she stared at me so fiercely I only managed to squeak out a small yes.

"From now on you may not tell anyone you want to be a witch," Nurse Harrigan said.

How was I supposed to find my Forever Family if I wasn't allowed to say I wanted to be a witch? I didn't want to be adopted by someone who didn't like witches by mistake, did I?

"But—"

"No buts, and no talking about witches! Have I made myself clear?"

I crossed my fingers behind my back, like Sam.

"Yes, Nurse Harrigan."

Over the next three years Sam decided he didn't want to be adopted by two more families because they didn't like animals and certainly not creepy crawly animals like lizards and worms. I decided not to be adopted by three different families because they just weren't right for me. The last family, the Bolsons, had been horrible and made me stay at the dining table until I'd eaten every single bit of brussels sprout and cabbage on my plate when I went to visit them for the day.

"Greens are good for you," they said.

I poked my fork in a bit of cold brussels sprout and wished it would disappear. I'd been sitting at the table for two hours!

I told Mrs. Bolson I'd put a spell on her so she got a warty nose, and then I told Mr. Bolson that I'd sprinkle mouse droppings on his cereal when he wasn't looking. They weren't so keen on adopting me after that. I certainly didn't want to be adopted by them.

I hadn't even wanted to visit the Bolsons in the first place. I'd been sure they weren't right for me, but Nurse Harrigan had said I should at least give them a try. "Sometimes people can surprise you," she said. Big mistake.

I began to wonder whether I would *ever* find my Forever Family.

"They must be out there somewhere," Sam said to me when I got back that night.

I wasn't so sure. Maybe my Forever Family didn't even exist, or maybe they'd adopted someone else by mistake and didn't need to adopt me any more.

But luckily that was just where I was wrong. Soon after, someone turned up at the children's home, someone who was completely different from anyone I'd ever met before.

As soon as I saw Lilith walking up the driveway I knew she was special and I wanted her to be special for me. I wanted Lilith to be my very own Forever Family, whatever it took.

Chapter 2

I raced down the stairs so fast that I was there by the time Maisie had opened the front door.

I was so excited I could hardly speak. The woman standing at the door smiled at me and it was as if I'd known her my whole life.

"Hello," I whispered.

"Hello, Bella Donna," she replied. "I'm Lilith."

She knew my name—and I hadn't even told it to her. How could she have known my name? Had Nurse Harrigan told her about me? Did Nurse Harrigan think that Lilith might want to adopt me? I hoped so. I really hoped so.

"I'll show you through to the matron's office," Maisie said.

"I can do that," I said, stepping quickly in front of Maisie.

Maisie looked confused. "Are you sure? You don't usually volunteer to do helpful things."

"Yes, I do!" I said. I did lots of helpful things all the time. Just not the helpful things Maisie *wanted* me to do, like making my bed and tidying my room.

Lilith smiled. "I'm sure you do," she said. "You probably just need to be asked to do the *right* helpful things. Ones that require your own unique special skills."

I wasn't quite sure what she meant. Unique special skills? I didn't think I had any of those.

Lilith was still smiling at me. I was sure that whatever she meant by "unique special skills" it was something good. I smiled back.

"My own unique special skills," I said. "Exactly."

I knocked on Nurse Harrigan's door and called out, "Visitor!"

Nurse Harrigan opened the door. She looked very pleased to see Lilith. "Miss Sorciere, won't you come in?" she said.

I followed Lilith inside. What an unusual name she had. I rolled it around my mouth like a delicious new flavor, trying it out—*Sor-syar, Sore-sea-air, Saw-c-err.*

"Not you," Nurse Harrigan said to me. "Just Miss Sorciere."

She showed Lilith to the comfy armchair

reserved for special guests and closed the door.

I sat down on the floor outside Nurse Harrigan's office. It was a bit cold but I didn't mind. I leaned against the door, crossed my fingers, and wished. "Please be my Forever Family, please be my Forever Family, please be my Forever Family."

From inside the office I could hear the murmur of voices but not the actual words they were saying.

Then Nurse Harrigan opened her office door so fast I almost fell inside.

"Isabella, what on earth are you doing out there?" she said, angrily.

"I was, um . . ."

"Bella, is that you?" Lilith said. "Come on in."

"I wasn't listening," I said. "You can't hear anything through that door."

"Bella Donna," Lilith said, and I knew she was going to say something very important. "Do you think you might be interested in being adopted by someone like me . . . ?"

"Yes, yes, yes, yes, yes!"

"I don't have a husband or any other children so I'm a bit worried you might be lonely . . ."

"I wouldn't be."

"I've got five cats. Do you like cats?"

"I love them," I said, although I hadn't really had anything much to do with cats as we didn't have pets at the children's home.

"How about a month's trial first?" said Nurse Harrigan. "To see how the two of you get along?"

"Perfect," said Lilith.

My grin was so huge it was almost too big to fit on my face.

"I'll pack my bags," I said.

"Not so fast," said Nurse Harrigan. "There's several weeks of paperwork and formalities to sort through first. You can't just wander off with anyone you feel like."

I wanted to tell her that Lilith was definitely not just *anyone*. But I didn't dare.

I ran up the stairs to the room I shared with three other girls, who weren't there because it was Sunday morning when everyone usually went swimming. As soon as I got in the room I let out the most enormous cheer of happiness.

"*YES!*"

And then I danced around and jumped on my bed a little bit, even though we are definitely not allowed to jump on the beds.

"What's going on?" Sam said, poking his head around the door. He'd decided not to go swimming because he wanted to look after an injured sparrow he'd found.

"My Forever Family came," I said. "Only she isn't a Forever Family. She's a Forever Person, and she's PERFECT."

A few weeks later the boring stuff was all done and the day had finally arrived when Lilith was coming to pick me up. I'd had my suitcase packed for ages. I was sitting on the wall outside the children's home waiting for her. Sam came to join me and just before Lilith arrived Nurse Harrigan and Maisie came out, too.

Lilith drove up in the most gorgeous red sports car I'd ever seen. The doors didn't even open like normal doors—they sort of lifted up.

"Wow!" I said.

"Like it?" she asked.

"Oh yes."

"Be very, very good," Nurse Harrigan warned me. "And no mention of *you know what*." She tapped the side of her nose with her index finger.

"I won't," I said. Even though it felt all wrong, I'd promised Nurse Harrigan I would never, not even once, mention that I wanted to be a witch.

I took my witch mobile with me, though. It would have a place of pride in my new room.

"This is for you," Sam said, and he gave me two of his favorite tiny toads. "You can set them free in your new garden."

"Thanks."

"How lovely," said Lilith. "Toads are one of my very favorite creatures."

"Mine, too," said Sam, beaming.

I knew Lilith was perfect.

"And this is for you," I said to Sam and gave him a blue feather pen that I'd gotten from the market. The sparrow he'd been looking after had flown away a few days before.

"Thanks," Sam said. I could tell he really liked the pen.

"We'll miss you," said Maisie, and she gave me a big hug.

"Really?" I said. I'd have thought Maisie would have been relieved that I was finally going.

"You're quite a character, Bella," Nurse Harrigan said, and she gave me a kiss on the cheek, which I didn't like very much, but I managed not to wipe off—I'd been told that it was rude.

"Ready?" said Lilith.

"Yes." I climbed into the sports car and the door closed all by itself.

I looked behind us as we sped down the street. Sam, Maisie, and Nurse Harrigan were waving. Sam looked sad. I hoped he'd find his own Forever Family soon.

🕷️🕷️🕷️

"Here we are," Lilith said, as she turned into Coven Road.

I was home.

Lilith was still talking. "It's called Coven Road but it isn't really a *road* as such, it's more of a cul-de-sac because there's only one way in and out."

"It's fantastic!" I said. I'd never seen anywhere like it before. Every house was different. I couldn't even tell how some of them were managing to stay up.

There was one house that looked like a miniature Taj Mahal. Another at the top of the

hill was like an ice palace with gold steps leading
up to it. There was a house balanced in a tree
like something Tarzan would have been proud
to call home, while another looked like it was
made from millions of different colored jewels.

"That one is like something from *Aladdin*,"
I said, and I smiled at Lilith. Coven Road was
going to be great!

For a second Lilith looked shocked. "Oh—
are you sure?" she said. "I didn't think . . ."

"What?" I asked, turning to her. But when I looked again all the wonderful houses had disappeared and Coven Road was a very ordinary crescent-shaped cul-de-sac of modern houses with a garden in the center.

"W–Where . . . What . . .?" I spluttered.

"This is my house," Lilith said, and we stopped outside a house that looked just the same as all the others.

I realized my imagination must have been playing tricks on me before—although it had all seemed so real. I blinked hard but the magical houses didn't reappear when I opened my eyes.

"Do you like it?" Lilith asked.

I couldn't disappoint her. "Perfect," I said, as I got out of the car. It was the perfect house for a perfectly ordinary girl—me—who was going to live a perfectly ordinary life.

I'd promised Nurse Harrigan there'd be no mention of spells or me wanting to be a witch and there wouldn't be.

Lilith's house was very, very ordinary indeed. I tried not to be disappointed—even though I was, just a little bit. Lilith was so special that I'd thought her house would be special, too.

I felt a bit mean. Ordinary was good. Ordinary was very, very good.

"It's just the way I hoped it would be," I said and smiled at Lilith.

"Well, that's good!" she said. "I'm glad you like it."

Before we went inside we went through the gate at the side that led to the back garden and set free the tiny toads that Sam had given me.

And then we went inside. Almost as soon as I'd gone through the door, a small black and gray striped cat with golden eyes ran over to me and started purring.

"That's Pegatha," Lilith laughed. "I think she's trying to say hello."

I crouched down and stroked the little cat. "Hello, Pegatha."

Pegatha purred.

The other four cats, all Siamese, looked very haughty and sat on the bookshelves.

"They're not as friendly as Pegatha," Lilith said.

I gave each of them a stroke but they didn't look as though they liked it much.

"What are their names?" I asked.

"Mystica, Bazeeta, Brimalkin, and Amelka," Lilith said. "Mystica's very old, Bazeeta and Brimalkin are brothers, and Amelka is Mystica's daughter."

She showed me to my room. It had cream walls with a poster of a kitten above the bed and one of a unicorn next to the door. The quilt was pink with white spots that made your eyes go a bit blurry if you stared at it for too long.

Pegatha jumped onto the bed and made herself at home.

"The flowers are from the garden," Lilith said, pointing to a small blue vase of slightly wilted purple and yellow pansies.

"They're lovely. Thank you." I felt a bit shy and emotional all of a sudden. I stroked Pegatha so Lilith wouldn't notice.

"Shall I leave you alone for a little while so you can unpack and get yourself settled?" Lilith asked me.

I nodded.

Once she'd gone, I took out my witch mobile and hung it in the window. I finally had a home and a bedroom of my own—only it wasn't the way I'd imagined it. I'd thought it would be more . . . more special. I tried not to be disappointed but I couldn't help it. So far the only thing that hadn't been ordinary was Lilith's car and her cats' names. A tear slipped down my face, and I wiped it away. I told myself not to be so ungrateful. What would Sam think if he could see me blubbing like a baby?

I was going to make the best of it. I'd been so very sure that Lilith was my Forever Family and I'd waited so long for her. I didn't want to be wrong.

Chapter 3

Over the next few days I met our neighbors in
Coven Road and the most unusual thing about
all of them was that they were so incredibly
ordinary. They were just what you'd expect
each and every one of them to be like. An

insurance man called Mr. Robson lived next door with his wife, Mrs. Robson, who smelled of roses. Mr. Robson didn't smell of anything particularly, but he had two strands of hair combed over his bald head that he kept patting and smoothing, as if he wanted to make sure they were still in place.

On the other side of us lived Mr. and Mrs. Turner and their little Yorkshire terrier called Waggy. Pegatha was the only one of Lilith's cats who went outside and she didn't like Waggy very much. Waggy wagged his tail

whenever he saw her and Pegatha's fur spiked along her back whenever she saw him.

Waggy was the only dog living in Coven Road. Lots of people had cats, though, so he was a bit outnumbered.

"Waggy's just trying to be friendly," I told Pegatha. But she didn't seem to agree.

The people living in the thirteen houses on Coven Road seemed to be as ordinary as the street itself. Even the postman, who delivered our mail on his bike, looked like a typical postman.

The only one who was a bit unusual was Lilith's niece, Verity.

She was a couple years older than me and lived with her mom at the far end of Coven Road. She went to the local middle school. Verity always dressed in black and had black hair and lots of black eyeliner around her eyes, like Cleopatra. I thought she looked fantastic.

"Hi," I said shyly, when she came around to visit.

"Welcome to Coven Road." Verity smiled. "It's nice to finally have someone around my own age living here."

She wanted to be my friend! I'd found my Forever Family and I'd made a friend! I was soooooo lucky!

Pegatha came into the room and hissed at Verity.

"Why does she always do that, Aunt Lilith?" Verity asked.

Lilith said she didn't know. "But I think cats are just like that. They do what they want when they want to and they like who they like—and that's that."

Pegatha jumped onto my lap and purred.

Lilith laughed.

"Charming!" Verity said, then laughed, too. "What's she got that I haven't, you silly cat?"

I liked it that Pegatha liked me so much. It felt as if she was *my* cat. At night, she crept into my room and curled up on my bed to sleep.

I'd never had a cat before and I thought Pegatha was *purrfect*!

My trial adoption was for one month. Just one month and then we'd decide if it should be permanent. I wanted it to be permanent *really* badly and I was going to do everything I could to make sure it was. I was determined to be the perfect girl and I made a list of all the things I thought a perfect girl would be like.

1. Well Behaved

A perfect girl would always be as good as gold.
No hair pulling, no scratching, no fighting.
No shouting out in class.

2. Good Manners

A perfect girl would eat quietly
with her mouth closed.

(Maisie was always scolding me for chewing loudly and letting everyone see what I was eating.)

She'd help old people across the street.

(But only if they wanted to be helped.)

3. Help Out Around the House

A perfect girl would make her bed every
single day and offer to do the dishes.

4. Homework
*A perfect girl would always do her
homework on time.*

5. Brussels Sprouts and Cabbage
*A perfect girl would eat brussels sprouts
and cabbage and not be sick.*

(But I really hoped Lilith didn't serve them
too often.)

I sucked on my pencil and tried to think
of the most perfect girl in my class at school
and came up with Angela. Angela was always
bringing our teacher apples and flowers and
she always, always, always wore pink.

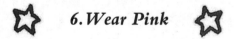

6. Wear Pink

If I stuck to my six simple rules, Lilith
would know I was the perfect girl to adopt—

no trouble at all. It was going to be difficult but I was going to do the very, very best I could.

✿✿✿

The next day Lilith took me clothes shopping at the mall. She said I could have anything I liked. There were some beautiful gothic clothes that I lingered over. I wanted them very much indeed—all dark and dramatic, like Verity would wear. But I didn't choose any of them.

I walked over to the pink clothes rack instead and chose some new clothes from it.

"Are you sure that's what you want?" Lilith frowned.

I nodded because I couldn't bring myself to lie and say yes out loud.

Lilith held the new clothes at arm's length, between her forefinger and thumb, as she placed them on the checkout counter.

I wore my pink clothes to school. "Are you sick?" Sam asked, when he saw my new look. "No." "Have you gone color blind then?" he said. "No—pink is a perfectly nice color," I told him. "I know it is for some people—lots of people. But you're Bella Donna, remember? The girl who wants to be a—"

"Shhh! Don't say it out loud," I told Sam, but he said it anyway.

". . . witch . . ."

Luckily no one heard him.

". . . for as long as I've known you and that's just about forever."

"So?" I said. Sam could be really annoying sometimes.

"So you should be wearing black as usual. Witches wear black."

And that made me really angry because of course I wanted to be wearing black.

"You don't know anything!" I shouted at him.

And then I remembered that perfect girls don't shout.

Sam looked hurt. "All right. Keep your hair on," he said.

"Hello. Are you new?" Angela said to me. And then her eyes opened really wide when she realized it was me. "But . . . but . . ."

I gave our teacher, Mrs. Pearce, the flowers I'd picked on the way to school and she looked just as shocked as Angela had. "Well, I never thought I'd see the day," she said.

"Here's my homework—all finished," I said, and I gave Mrs. Pearce my math book.

"Are you feeling all right, Bella?" she asked me.

"Perfect," I told her. All I had to do was keep this up for a few more weeks and Lilith would adopt me.

The other girls at school started to be much nicer to me.

Angela sat with me at lunch and watched as I opened my new pink lunchbox and took out a strawberry jam sandwich and started to eat it slowly and politely, with my mouth tightly closed.

I'd tried telling Lilith I'd like to only have pink food from now on but she hadn't been impressed. She'd let me have a strawberry jam sandwich for that day but she said only eating pink food was most unwise. And I agreed. There were so many nice foods of other colors.

"No slug sandwiches today then?" Angela said. It was a feeble joke, but Sam, who was sitting at the table behind us, was outraged.

"Eating slugs is cruel," he said. "Slugs have feelings, you know."

"Yeah, right, Slug Boy," another boy at Sam's table said, laughing. "He's such an idiot."

"No I'm not!"

I wanted to punch and kick them for being mean to Sam. But I didn't want to get in trouble for fighting. A perfect girl never fights. I swallowed the rest of my perfectly chewed sandwich.

"You're different," Angela said.

"Am I?"

"Yes—much nicer than you used to be. I think I could even be your friend now."

"Great." Angela would be the perfect friend for a perfect girl.

Sam got up from the table and ran off. I was going to run after him and say sorry for being mean to him earlier, but some of the other girls in my class wanted me to join in their game.

It was the first time I'd ever been asked to play and I didn't want to say no.

It felt strange when other girls in my class invited me to sit with them in the afternoon. Strange, but nice, too.

Trying to be perfect had turned me from unpopular into popular and it was a lot easier to be popular. I liked people liking me. I liked wearing pink.

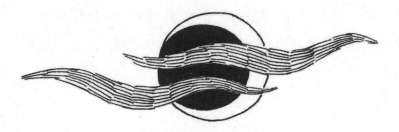

Chapter 4

Over the next week, Angela invited me to her house after school twice. Ellen and Rajni picked me to sit next to them in class. In PE I always used to be the last one to get chosen for any teams but not any more. Now the other girls looked pleased to have me on their team rather than sighing loudly when the teacher told them they had to have me. My newfound popularity was great.

But sometimes, when I really thought about it, I felt a tiny bit sad. I'd changed into this whole new person that wasn't really me. Only everyone seemed to like her much better than the real me.

Just because I looked different and chewed politely and didn't fight and would have eaten brussels sprouts (but luckily Lilith didn't serve any) and helped old people across the road (but no old people needed help when I was walking past) and tried to be as much like Angela as I could, it shouldn't have made such a big difference.

I was still me, wasn't I?

Even Lilith seemed to like the new me.

"What a helpful girl you've turned out to be," she'd say, when I offered to do the dishes, again.

I'd been living with Lilith for two weeks and it was starting to get hard to remember what it used to be like when I was living at the children's home. In the mornings, she'd always make something nice for breakfast and she was always cheerful and seemed really pleased that I was there living with her.

I had to leave for school, usually on the new pink bike Lilith had bought me as a surprise, before she went to work. I wasn't exactly sure what Lilith did for her job but she was always home by the time I got back. I thought she might have worked in insurance with Mr. Robson from next door. I tried asking her but she just said, "Oh, let's not talk about my boring day. Let's talk about you instead. What have you been up to?"

My favorite times were when it was just the two of us and the cats, which was how it usually was. Lilith loved to cook and I loved helping her. One day we tried baking some special homemade cat treats—cheesy ones and then chicken ones. Pegatha stayed close to us in the kitchen and looked like she was sniffing the smells coming from the oven. When Lilith took the treats out of the oven, Pegatha purred happily. I laughed and laughed.

She was so funny. "You can't have them yet, they're too hot," I told her.

Pegatha would have eaten all the treats herself if she could have, but Mystica, Bazeeta, Brimalkin, and Amelka had to have some, too. At first they turned their noses up at them but then Brimalkin had a taste and couldn't resist. He gobbled his up while the other three looked on snootily—and then they gobbled up theirs as well.

I liked living with Lilith so much that I told myself it didn't matter that I still hadn't told her I wanted to be a witch. Because I hadn't told her right away, I soon found I couldn't tell her at all. I was sure she was supposed to be my Forever Person but could I have made a mistake? Was my Forever Family still out there somewhere, waiting for me?

No, no, no. I wanted it to be Lilith. I didn't want to live with anyone else.

Sometimes at school I saw Sam looking sad. He always seemed to look sad these days.

"Templeton isn't the same now you're not there," he said. Sam was the oldest one left.

"Your Forever Family's got to come soon," I told him.

He shrugged. "Do you ever wonder if perhaps we shouldn't have made that pact when we were five? That there's not always exactly the right person out there and that *nearly right* might do?"

I didn't know. I'd always been so sure before but I wasn't quite so sure any more.

Sometimes I felt like I was an actor playing a part, pretending to be someone I wasn't. It wasn't sticking to the six rules that was the problem—it was not telling Lilith the truth about wanting to be a witch.

"You okay, Bella?" Lilith asked me one day, and I almost told her but chickened out.

"Yes, yes, I'm fine," I said.

"Because if there was something troubling you, you'd tell me, wouldn't you?"

"Of course I would," I lied, stroking Pegatha.

Pegatha curled up on my pillow when it was time to go to sleep.

"What am I going to do, Pegatha? What am I going to do?" I whispered. I felt so guilty for not telling Lilith the truth.

Pegatha didn't have any answers besides a purr or two.

It was midnight and I still couldn't sleep. I looked out the window and couldn't believe my eyes. There was a rainbow arching across the night sky, weaving in and out of the stars. It was so beautiful, but it couldn't be real, could it? There couldn't really be a rainbow at night. Rainbows needed the sun.

I ran down the hallway to Lilith's room.

"Lilith!" I cried, bursting in.

Lilith woke up with a start. "Huh? What—what is it? Are you all right, Bella Donna? What's wrong?"

I pulled back the curtains. "Look!" I said.

But the rainbow's colors weren't as powerful as they were before and by the time Lilith had come to the window it had faded away.

"It was right there!"

"What was?"

"A night rainbow."

"Are you sure? Rainbows happen when the sun shines in the rain. Perhaps you were dreaming?"

"No, I was awake."

Pegatha whirled herself around and around my legs, purring, and I got distracted. Could it have been a dream after all?

"Try to go back to sleep," Lilith said, as she tucked me back into bed. "Shall I take Pegatha away? Maybe she's keeping you awake."

But I liked having Pegatha with me. "No, let her stay. Please."

"All right, if you're sure. Good night, Bella."

"Night, Lilith."

After school the next day, Verity came over with something from her mom for Lilith. I asked Verity about the rainbow but she only looked over at Lilith, who shook her head, and then Verity laughed.

"A rainbow? You saw a rainbow at night?"

"Yes."

"Shining among the stars?"

"Yes—I told you."

"I think you might need glasses," Verity said to me.

"But I can see everything else fine," I said quietly.

Lilith invited Verity to stay for dinner and Verity said yes, please. I think she'd have liked to come to our house every day, if she could. Her mom was always working and didn't get home until late.

"Then there's only one explanation," Verity continued, as she set the table with me.

"What's that?" I asked her.

"You've gone loopy. No one would ever see anything as magical as a night rainbow in a street as ordinary as Coven Road."

But the next day, a Friday, we all got sent home early because there'd been an outbreak of something nasty at school. And that was when everything changed.

That afternoon when I walked down Coven Road it looked different. So different I thought I must have taken a wrong turn. Where were the thirteen ordinary modern houses I was used to seeing? The street sign definitely said COVEN ROAD. But now the road had a house that Aladdin would have been proud to come home to and one next door to that which Tarzan would have liked. The garden in the center of the cul-de-sac was full of exotic plants and I'm sure I saw a real live pink flamingo—although it could have been plastic, I suppose.

I pinched myself to make sure I wasn't dreaming. No, definitely awake. I could feel my heart thumping ultra fast.

I couldn't see our house right away because it was tucked in, just after Aladdin's and Tarzan's. But when I could see it, I saw that it looked completely different, too. Where our old house used to be, there was this amazing

thatched cottage with roses around the door. Every now and again one or other of the roses, which looked exactly like real roses and smelled like real roses, too, changed color from turquoise to gold to red to pink to yellow to

lilac. It was like a house from a fairy tale. I went up the garden path. At least Pegatha hadn't changed. She was basking in the sunshine on the windowsill.

But was it really Pegatha? Was it really our house? I felt a bit scared. Would Lilith have changed? Would she be indoors waiting for me as she usually was? Maybe I should ring the doorbell rather than letting myself in with my key. Then I saw the door was ajar so I pushed it open.

Our house looked just the same as usual inside but it didn't smell the same. Lilith must have been making something very odd for dinner.

I could hear her singing to herself in the kitchen.

As I got closer, I saw that Lilith was stirring a black cauldron as she added ingredients to it. And she wasn't singing like she normally did—she was chanting. She was chanting a spell . . . just like a . . .

"You're a witch!" I exclaimed.

Lilith dropped the wooden spoon she'd been using to stir the cauldron with a clatter.

"Oh—oh—oh, I'm sorry. I didn't mean for you to find out," she said.

"Didn't mean . . .?"

"You seemed so happy being a perfectly ordinary girl. I knew I'd have to tell you one day, but it's not always easy being a witch and so I thought I'd wait. And you seemed so happy . . ."

"I wasn't," I said.

Lilith looked surprised. "Weren't you?"

"No—well, yes, sort of . . . but all I really wanted was to be a witch. Only I couldn't say so, so I tried to be the perfect girl instead."

"Why couldn't you say?"

"Because I promised Nurse Harrigan."

"Oh. So all this time you wanted to be a witch—just like me?"

"Just like you," I said, smiling at her.

Lilith smiled back. "I should have guessed. You were just pretending to be normal?"

"Yes, and it didn't feel right. I'm sorry I didn't tell you the truth."

"No, it's me who should be sorry for not telling you right away, only I was trying to be more normal, too—for you."

And then Lilith and I started laughing and laughing. We laughed so hard I thought we'd never stop. We were laughing so hard tears streamed down our faces.

"Did you always want to be a witch, then?" Lilith asked.

"Yes," I told her. "I've wanted to be one for as long as I can remember, which is right back to when I was a baby. My witch mobile was the only thing that was left with me on the doorstep of the children's home when I was a baby."

I had so many questions I wanted to ask Lilith. So many things I needed her to explain to me.

"Why . . . why is Coven Road different today? It's like the first time I saw it."

"It's a spell," said Lilith. "And it usually starts working at the time you come home from school—but you're early today. Everyone has to help cast it at midnight once a month. No one who isn't a witch must ever see the real Coven Road. Not that we get many visitors, being a cul-de-sac. And of course there's the misdirection spell, too—a non-witch walking by Coven Road wouldn't even notice it was here. They'd just walk right past it."

"But I find it every day," I said.

"Yes—but . . ."

"But what?"

"You're not a normal girl, Bella. You might not know how to cast spells yet, but anyone on Coven Road can see . . ."

My heart was beating fast. I thought I knew what she was going to say. But it couldn't be true, could it?

"See what?" I asked.

And finally Lilith said the words I wanted to hear: "You're a witch."

It was true then. Somehow I'd always known. But now she'd said it out loud! It really was true. I really was a witch!

"You said *everyone* on Coven Road?"

"Oh yes, everyone on Coven Road is a witch," Lilith said. "Strictly speaking, male witches are called warlocks, but we always call ourselves witches."

"What, so even Mr. and Mrs. Robson are witches?"

Lilith smiled and nodded.

"And Mr. and Mrs. Turner?" They couldn't be witches, too, could they?

"Of course," said Lilith.

"And Waggy?"

"No, he's just a dog."

"And Verity—is Verity a witch, too?"

"Yes—she's known as a witchling because she's a young witch in training."

A witchling. It sounded so good.

"Am I a witchling?"

"Well, you could be—if you let me train you in spell-casting."

"Oh yes—yes, please, I'd like that very much." I thought I might like it more than anything in the world.

Lilith smiled. "Good. I've wanted to show you how to cast spells ever since I overheard a woman called Mrs. Bolson, who had a large wart on her nose, complaining about a child called Bella Donna from Templeton Children's Home. 'That wretched child said she'd give me a warty nose and now look what's happened!'"

"That was me! I did say I'd give her a warty nose. I didn't know it would really work!"

I wondered how many other things that I'd said or wished had come true and I hadn't even known.

It didn't work every time. I remembered sitting at the kitchen table at the Bolsons' house wishing that the cold brussels sprout on the end of my fork would disappear. But it hadn't.

"Lilith, do you like brussels sprouts?"

"Not much—do you?"

"Not much either. That's a relief. How about cabbage?"

"Not stewed cabbage but I like raw white and red cabbage in coleslaw."

"Oh—me, too. So could you tell I was a witch from the first time you saw me?"

"I was pretty sure but not absolutely. As I walked up Templeton Drive I hoped that perhaps, if I was very lucky, I might have found a witch child. But then, well, you seemed so happy being ordinary. And I started to think you'd like me more if you thought I was an ordinary woman, too, and so that's what I pretended to be. Although I could see as soon as I met you that you were anything but ordinary. Now we must have a Welcome to the Real Coven Road ceremony for you."

"For me? I don't need a special ceremony."

It was enough just to know I was witch and Lilith was a witch, too—and she was going to teach me how to cast spells. And best of all we didn't have to pretend or tell lies to each other ever again.

But Lilith insisted. "Yes, you do need a ceremony. You must. It's tradition and once you've been to the ceremony then you truly are a witch of Coven Road and must uphold the witches' code—there'll be no going back."

I knew I would never want to go back.

"Anyway," Lilith added, "I've never met a witch that didn't love getting dressed up—any excuse will do. Sunset tonight should be time enough for everything to be prepared."

Chapter 5

Number seven Coven Road now appeared as a magnificent Ice Palace where the leader of all the witches, the Grand Sorceress Zorellda, lived, and where my official Welcome to the Real Coven Road ceremony was to be held.

I had on a long purple gown and Lilith wore a deep blue one. She'd also threaded some purple flowers through my hair.

"You'll need to go up onto the stage," Lilith told me as we walked there. "Zorellda will tell you what the three rules are and you must promise to stick to them."

"Okay," I said. It didn't sound too hard.

Lilith frowned. "These aren't just any rules, like at school. These are rules that *absolutely* must not be broken."

I nodded.

From the outside, the Ice Palace looked magnificent with twirling turrets and a fountain with miniature dancing pink dolphins swimming in it. It looked especially magnificent as the sun was setting and a golden glow shone on everything.

Inside, the Ice Palace was even more splendid with paintings on the ceiling and stained glass windows. It was warm, not cold as I'd expected an Ice Palace to be. The Great Hall was full by the time Lilith and I got there. Previously, everyone on Coven Road had looked ordinary, but now they were all wearing weird and wonderful clothes.

My mouth hung open as I saw a man with long, feathery, blue hair and a coat that looked like it was made from silver spiders— although it wasn't exactly "made" because the spiders were all still alive and moving around. Creepy. The man saw me looking at him and winked and I realized it was Mr. Turner from next door!

I felt a bit scared that I was going to have to go up onto the stage in front of them all.

Lilith squeezed my hand. "You'll be fine," she said.

"I hope I don't fall over or do something stupid," I whispered back.

"Good luck," said Verity, coming over to us.

I breathed a sigh of relief. At least she still looked like herself, although, being Verity, she looked more gorgeous than ever in a red ball gown, long black gloves, and a black top hat with a ginormous ruby in the middle of it.

A huge bell started to ring.

"That bell's only used for special occasions," Verity said, "and emergencies."

"Everyone is here—time to take our seats," Lilith said to me.

Verity gave me a thumbs up sign.

Lilith steered me to two seats in the front row that had been especially reserved for us.

When everyone was seated, the bell stopped ringing and it was so quiet you could have heard a pin drop. I felt like sneezing but managed to stop myself by squeezing my nostrils hard.

Zorellda walked onto the stage and everyone clapped. I'd never seen the Grand Sorceress before.

She looked very old, maybe even as old as a hundred, with long white hair that was swept up high. She wore long eggshell blue robes and had piercing golden eyes.

"We are gathered here to welcome our newest resident, Bella Donna," Zorellda said, looking toward me.

I could feel myself blushing.

Lilith gave me a little push, "Go on," she said, nodding at the stage.

It was time for me to go out front. My legs felt wobbly as I stood up.

It seemed to take forever to walk up the nine steps to the stage. All the way I could feel eyes staring at me, and I didn't like it much.

I stood under an enormous chandelier that was lit by candles with flames that changed color as they burned.

"Bella Donna," Zorellda said. Her golden eyes stared into mine and it felt like she was seeing right into the heart of me and knew every part of what there was to know and would be to know about me. "Do you promise to obey the three laws of Coven Road?"

I nodded my head, but that wasn't enough.

"To each question you must answer, 'I promise'," she said.

"Okay."

"Do you promise never to tell anyone who isn't a witch about Coven Road?" Zorellda asked.

"I promise."

"And do you promise never to use magic outside Coven Road—apart from in the direst of circumstances?"

"I promise."

"And finally, do you promise never to bring anyone who isn't a witch to Coven Road, without prior permission from myself?"

"I promise."

"And should you break any of the promises you will accept the consequence—banishment from Coven Road."

I definitely wasn't going to break any of the promises—not ever. I wasn't sure if I was supposed to say "I promise" again but it obviously didn't matter. Zorellda had turned to everyone else.

"Please stand," she said.

There was rustling and chair-scraping as everyone stood up.

"You have all heard Bella Donna's promises?"

"We have," replied every voice in the hall.

"And you will all do everything you can to help her keep them?"

"We will," the voices said.

"Then let the party begin," said Zorellda.

Witches' parties are the most amazing, fantastic, wilder-than-wild events. This party was held outside—Lilith said the weather was always perfect on Coven Road—partly in the street and partly in the exotic garden in the center of the cul-de-sac.

Lilith put a spell on my bedroom rug that
turned it into a magic carpet and then she let

me fly on it out of the window and up and down Coven Road.

"Hello," cried a voice, and I looked around to see the postman flying on a magic carpet, too. "Much easier than riding a bike," he called, as he whizzed past me. "Although not as healthy!"

It was like no party I'd ever been to before—there were fireworks flying through the air that never went out, snake charming, fire eating, and people laughing everywhere. The garden in the center had two unicorns in it and there were tiny elephants about the size of cats. I was sure there was lots more to see and I was looking forward to exploring.

"Now we can be real friends, no secrets," Verity said. She was swinging on one of the magical swings in the garden. It had daisy chains to hold onto and stayed in the air without being attached to any metal bars or to the ground. Hundreds of butterflies flew around it.

She jumped off the swing.

"Come on—I'm starving." She dragged me over to the buffet table where there was every sort of food imaginable. And if you did manage to imagine something you especially liked that wasn't on the table, then that magically appeared on the table, too!

"Go on, think of something that isn't there," Verity said.

It was hard to think of anything because every time I thought of something, I found it there already. Plus, I wasn't hungry. But Verity was waiting to see what I'd come up with.

"Strawberry . . ." I said.

A plate of strawberries appeared.

"Um . . . chocolate . . ."

Bars and boxes of every sort of chocolate piled themselves high beside the strawberries.

". . . ice . . ."

A pile of ice formed next to the strawberries.

". . . cream."

The strawberries, ice, and chocolate suddenly turned into an enormous bowl of strawberry ice cream, streaked with chocolate sauce.

Verity laughed at my shocked face. "Great, isn't it?" She ladled out a glass of something green and bubbly for me. I didn't really want to taste it but she said it was spell juice so I took a sip. It tasted like nothing I'd ever tasted before. Nice but strange. Thick and thin at the same time.

"I wish Sam could be here," I said. "His eyes would pop out if he could see all this."

"Who's Sam?" Verity asked.

"An old friend from the children's home. He hasn't found his Forever Family yet."

Not like me, I thought. I'd found mine.

Sam would love being here. He'd especially like the unicorns in the garden and he wouldn't believe Mr. Turner's spider coat! But I knew I mustn't tell him about all this. I'd made a promise and I was going to keep it. I didn't want to be banished.

At midnight, a huge cauldron was lit at the top of the hill. It was time for the illusion and misdirection spell-casting.

As soon as the cauldron started to bubble, each witch threw in some ingredients. They looked mostly like flowers and twigs and herbs.

Lilith gave me a small muslin pouch with what smelled like lavender inside it.

"Throw it in," she said, pointing to the cauldron. And I did.

Then Zorellda started to chant and we all had to chant, too. I'm not sure if I pronounced the words right but I did my best.

"*Azhelma makara resanza delfar,*" I said, or something like that.

At the end of the spell-casting I suddenly felt sleepy. Really, really sleepy. It had been a very long and very, very exciting day.

When I woke up the next morning, I thought it might all have been a dream. But then I saw my bedroom rug wasn't where it usually was and jumped out of bed.

I could have moved the rug myself by accident, so I walked slowly over to the window and pulled open the curtains. Coven Road was still its wonderful, magical self! I jumped back into bed and pulled the covers over me. I was glad it was Saturday and I could sleep in. Pegatha crept up the bed and pushed my nose with her paw. "Ouch!"

"Bella," Lilith called from downstairs. "Come and have some breakfast and then we can start spell lessons."

Spell lessons! I was going to have spell lessons. It may have been Saturday, but this was a whole different type of school! This was the type of school where I wouldn't dawdle to class. This was the type of school where I'd always be the first one there and the last one to leave and I'd never miss a single lesson—even if I was sick.

I showered and dressed faster than I'd ever done before and raced down the stairs.

Lilith was looking through the pages of a special book called a grimoire. I loved saying it really, reaaaallllly slowly— *"grimm-wharrrr."* It even sounded magical! It was very, very old and had lots of spells in it. Some of the spells had been written down by Lilith but most of them had been written by other witches. Lilith had told me she'd been given the grimoire by her mom on her thirteenth birthday. Lilith's grandmother had given it to Lilith's mom and Lilith's great-grandmother had given it to Lilith's grandmother. And back and back it went for as long as there'd been witches in Lilith's family.

"You got ready quickly," Lilith said, looking up at me.

"Yes," I said, breathlessly. "Very quick."

As I tucked into my second blueberry pancake and wondered what spells I'd be learning, the doorbell rang.

"Oh good," said Lilith, going to the door.

Verity was there.

"You mean . . ." I said, looking at Verity. Was she going to learn how to cast spells, too?

"You didn't think you could have the best witchling teacher in the world all to yourself, did you?" Verity asked.

"No," I said. Only I had thought the spell lessons were going to be something Lilith and I were going to do together—just the two of us. Just me and Lilith. But perhaps it would be more fun with Verity joining in.

Pegatha hissed at Verity.

"Good morning to you, too!" Verity said.

Mystica, Bazeera, Brimalkin, and Amelka were on the bookshelves as usual, watching.

"Shall I get out the cauldron?" Verity said to Lilith. Then she turned back to me. "You keep eating—I can always do a few spells on my own with Lilith."

There was no way I was going to let Verity learn any spell-casting without me!

"Finished," I said, gulping down almost the whole of the last pancake in one swallow.

Chapter 6

"Have you ever wondered what it might be like to look like someone different or to be someone or something different?" Lilith asked us.

"Yes," I said.

"Yes," said Verity.

She'd been learning spells for a few years already. I was sure she must know lots of fantastic ones.

"What would you like to be, Bella Donna?" Lilith asked me.

"A witch!" I said.

"You're already a witch, or at least a witchling," said Verity.

I thought harder. "Would it be permanent?" I asked. Being something different for a short time wasn't the same as being stuck as something different forever.

"It can be for as long or as short as you like," said Lilith. "But you'd need to be near water if you wanted to be a fish . . ."

". . . and not be a mouse around the cats," added Verity.

"No," said Lilith. "That wouldn't be a good idea!"

Pegatha jumped onto my lap and purred at me.

"I think she's already thinking you'd make a good mouse," Verity said, laughing.

"Maybe we should start with something smaller," Lilith said. "A small appearance change."

"Purple hair," I said. "Long purple hair."

"Okay," said Lilith. "Long purple hair it is. I think purple hair will suit you. Repeat the words after me and make sure you imagine yourself with long purple hair at the same time."

There were shelves of ingredients throughout the room and Lilith dropped some herbs and poured some potions into the bubbling cauldron. A strong smell, not too unpleasant but not really nice either, wafted around the kitchen.

The spell words Lilith said were strange and hard to pronounce. They sounded a bit like, *"Eeerooola eeeroolu mooozlar kal."*

I had to repeat them three times while stirring the cauldron clockwise and imagining my purple hair as clearly as I could.

"Oh, that is nice," Lilith said, and she picked up a mirror to show me what I looked like.

It had worked! My hair had turned purple. Not a deep or a bright purple but it had a definite purple tinge to it and it was a few inches longer, too.

"A very good first spell," Lilith said and she smiled at me. I felt really, really happy—both because I'd made Lilith happy and because it had WORKED.

"Suppose we didn't want to change our own appearance," Verity said. "Suppose we wanted to change someone else's?"

"To change someone else you'd think about them instead of yourself while you were casting the spell. And of course you'd need to have something of theirs—usually a strand of hair works well, but it could be a piece of their clothing or jewelry, something like that."

It was Verity's turn. She gave herself long golden hair that stretched all the way down to the ground.

She really was amazing at spell-casting.

"What happens if a spell works too well?" I said. "What if Verity's hair had kept on growing and growing until it went right out the door?"

"That's why we have witchling lessons," Lilith told us. "The important thing for witchlings to master is doing magic when you mean to do it. I'm sure you've had occasions when you've felt so strongly about something that you've unexpectedly found that you've cast a spell."

"Is that why Mrs. Bolson got a warty nose and my nursery school teacher got black paint all over her when she said she didn't like witches?" I asked.

"Could be," Lilith said. "Spell-casting is an art rather than a science. You can't always guarantee the outcome.

"To reverse a spell you simply stir the cauldron counterclockwise and say the words backwards," Lilith continued.

"Simple," said Verity, as we tried just that.

Witchlings were only allowed to learn one new spell each week, so we practiced changing our appearance again. Verity gave herself pointed pixie ears and I gave myself sparkling silver shoes. Then Verity gave herself a long beard, which made me laugh and laugh because she looked so funny.

At the end of the lesson, Lilith gave Verity and me a small muslin bag each, about the size of a large marble, filled with the ingredients we'd used for the spell. I turned mine into a pendant and wore it around my neck. I wasn't going to take it off—apart from when I was in the shower or went swimming. My first spell-casting kit! I was so lucky.

"Why don't you invite Verity for a sleepover tonight?" Lilith suggested quietly as Verity was about to leave.

I'd never had a sleepover or been invited to one, although Sam and I had once had a midnight picnic in our den (it was just a packet of chocolate cookies, really), and I thought it was a great idea.

I asked Verity if she'd like to come over that night and she said she would. I was so happy.

Having Lilith for my Forever Family was wonderful. And being a witch's daughter was the most wonderful thing in the whole world. I still wanted to be the perfect girl but I crossed out number six on my list and wrote *Wear Black* instead and I crossed out number five and wrote, *Learn How to Be a Witchling*.

My witch mobile hung in the window and danced around in the breeze.

When Verity arrived we made popcorn and watched a movie and then we just talked and laughed. I told her all about being left on the doorstep of the children's home with only the witch mobile to my name and about Sam and me and how we'd waited for our Forever Families and how Sam was still waiting for his.

I'd never had a best friend before, unless you counted Sam and I'd known him forever, so he was more like a brother. Verity was really exciting. She was just the same as me—a witchling. Sam was more . . . more of a lizard and bug king.

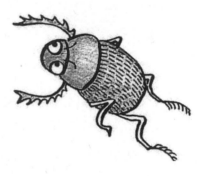

When I'd finished telling her everything, Verity gave a huge yawn. "Shall we go to sleep now?"

"Okay," I said, although I wasn't really all that sleepy. I was much too excited. I wanted to ask her lots of questions. I wanted to know what it was like being a witchling and about all the spells she'd learned.

"Night," Verity said.

I'd thought we were going to stay up for hours and I was disappointed that she wanted to go to sleep already. I bet Angela would have wanted to stay up all night. But I couldn't invite her or Rajni or Ellen around without Zorellda's permission because they weren't witches.

"Night." I pulled the pink and white spotted quilt up around my shoulders. "Verity . . ."

"Mmmm?"

"I'm so lucky to have you for a friend."

"You're so lucky to have Aunt Lilith for your mom," Verity said, as she punched her pillow to make it more comfy.

I fell asleep thinking how my life was now so great I sometimes had to pinch myself just in case it was all a dream. Although, if it was all a dream, then I definitely, definitely didn't want to wake up—not ever.

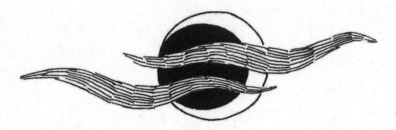

Chapter 7

On Monday morning I opened my wardrobe and tried to decide what to wear. Just about everything in it was now pink, and my new number six rule was to wear black.

"Are you all right, Bella Donna?" Lilith asked, coming into my room to see me standing there, gazing at my clothes.

"There's too much pink in here!" I told her.

Lilith smiled and produced something from behind her back. It was one of the gothic outfits I'd admired at the mall—a long black lace skirt and top. I quickly put it on. It fit me perfectly.

"Thank you," I gasped, looking at my reflection in the mirror. I looked like me again. I hadn't seen Lilith buy the outfit when we'd been shopping. She must have gone back to the store afterwards.

I tucked my spell pendant beneath my top and pulled out my favorite boots—black, flat, and with laces up the front.

Now I felt totally like my real self again.

"Good, you're back to being you," Sam said, as I walked through the school gates in my new outfit. "Although you're starting to look like a Cheshire cat," Sam told me.

"What's that?" I asked, wondering if Pegatha might be a Cheshire cat.

"Someone who grins a lot," Sam said, but he sounded happy for me.

"Any FF news?" I asked him.

The last two families that had wanted to adopt Sam, before I'd left, had definitely not been the right ones. The first family had been allergic to animals and Sam couldn't  live without any animals. The second family had won The Tidiest

House in Town competition three times in a row. Sam would have found it impossible to be tidy all the time. It was hard enough for him to manage a whole day without messing up his clothes or losing his shoes or getting covered in mud.

"Maybe," Sam said. "I haven't told anyone yet because I don't want to jinx it."

"You can tell me, though!"

Sam grinned. "Nurse Harrigan said she'd had an inquiry from a couple who run a woodland wildlife sanctuary nearby. They're coming to visit Templeton on Sunday."

"That'd be perfect!" I said.

"Yes, it would," said Sam. "If they like me."

"Of course they'll like you."

"Roll on the weekend," Sam said. His eyes were shining—he was so looking forward to meeting the Woodland Wildlifers.

"Yes, I can't wait either," I agreed, even though I couldn't tell him that for me the weekend meant witchling classes and spell-casting.

I was a little nervous about going into the classroom. I wasn't sure how the other girls in my class would react to me now I'd gone back to wearing black. Would they still want to be my friend? I hoped they would but I wasn't sure.

"Hi," I said to Angela, as I walked into class.

"Oh no," said Angela. "Not all that black again, Bella. I just knew it would happen one day." She opened her bag and pulled out a scrunchy with a pink flower on it. "Wear this so you can at least still be a little bit pink."

"Thanks," I said, and put the scrunchy in my hair. "Still friends?"

"Still friends," she said. "Even though you are a little bit weird."

Rajni and Ellen still wanted to be my friends, too. Rajni even asked me where I'd got my gothic clothes from at lunchtime—I still used my pink lunchbox. So long as I didn't accidentally use my magic or accidentally tell anyone about Coven Road, being a witch at a regular school was going to be fine.

Verity was sitting on one of the magic flower swings in the center garden of Coven Road when I got home. I guessed her mom wasn't back from work yet, as usual. After the sleepover, she'd wanted to stay at our house all day Sunday but I still went for swimming lessons with Sam and the other children from Templeton and Lilith had told Verity she had to go home.

I sat on the swing next to Verity and told her about my day and Sam's good news.

For the rest of the week I was a regular girl at school and a witchling at home—although really I was a witchling, and proud of it, all the time.

Not that things had really changed. Although the houses remained magical to my eyes, our life at home was pretty much the same as it had been before—mainly Lilith, Pegatha, the other cats, and me living happily together. But all week I waited desperately for Saturday and our next witchling lesson. I was almost too excited to sleep on Friday night.

At the start of the next spell lesson, Verity fetched the cauldron and Pegatha came to sit on my lap. The other cats stayed on the shelves.

I might have been near the bottom of the class in just about everything at regular school, but I'd taken to learning how to be a witchling like a duckling takes to water.

I don't know why, but whereas things I was told at school seemed to go in one ear and out the other, when it came to spells I was able to remember them and so far all the spells I'd tried—one to be exact—had worked.

"Let's try the moving spell today," Lilith said. She taught us how to make small things— like pencils and pens—move from one place to another. It didn't really need the cauldron but Lilith lit it and put some nice smelling stuff in it to help the class atmosphere.

The chant sounded something like, "*Hmmmmarty hmmmmrraaa hazaaaa.*"

"That was amazing," Verity said, after she'd chanted and made an apple wobble across the table.

"Yes it was—you're really coming along, Verity," said Lilith.

Verity looked very pleased with herself.

Lilith and I played a game moving Sam's feathery pen back and forth. He'd loaned it to me and I'd brought it home by mistake. We didn't touch the pen once—it was just the spell that made it move.

Pegatha wanted to play with it, too, but I told her she mustn't because I had to give it back to Sam on Monday.

At the end of the lesson, Verity volunteered to clean out the cauldron.

"Oh no, that's all right," Lilith said. Cleaning out the cauldron, depending on what had been put in it, could sometimes be a tedious job.

But Verity insisted we let her do it so Lilith and I went out into the garden to see if we could spot the toads that Sam had given me. We looked everywhere but we couldn't find them.

"They may have even moved on to another garden," Lilith said.

"Or gone to try to find Sam." All sorts of creatures seemed to like Sam. I just hoped the Woodland Wildlifers would like him, too.

Chapter 8

I was having a lovely dream about flying on a broomstick through the sky and doing loop the loops when a strange ringing sound interrupted me and nearly made me fall off the bed.

It was the telephone.

I tried to ignore it but I couldn't because now I was wide awake and it went on ringing. I went downstairs and picked up the receiver.

"Hello?"

It was Sam and he was in such a state and talking so fast I could hardly understand him.

"They'll never . . . forever . . . now no one . . . I'll . . . awful . . ."

"What? Sam—just slow down," I told him.

But he wouldn't listen to me. It was early Sunday morning—the day he was going to meet the Woodland Wildlifers. It was the day Sam had been waiting for, well, forever!

"What's happened?"

"My face!"

"What about your face?"

"Mess."

The pressure of meeting his Forever Family must have been too much for him. I didn't understand what had happened but it was clear he wanted a friend and I'd been too busy to be much of a friend recently. He needed me.

"I'm coming over," I told him. "Just stay next to the phone."

The phone at Templeton was just by the main door.

"Can't stay here," he said.

"Then where?"

"Den."

"What—no, wait!"

Too late. He'd put down the phone.

I pulled my coat on over my pajamas and pushed my feet into my boots. They weren't very comfortable without socks and made funny sounds when I walked.

I looked back up the stairs. Lilith was still asleep and I didn't want to wake her so I left a note: *Gone to see Sam. Back soon.*

I pedalled my bike through the deserted early morning streets to Templeton and went around the back to where the old greenhouse was.

"Sam," I called out. "Sam!"

I pushed open the old greenhouse door. He was lucky it didn't just fall down on top of him, it was so rickety.

"Bella," said a small, very sad voice. "Look at me."

Sam was in a state. I'd never seen a rash that looked quite as nasty as this one before. It wasn't just pimples, like measles or chicken pox. The spots were much bigger, more like boils really, and some of them were yellow and some were greenish and some were red and sore. One or two were even blue. Weird—and revolting.

"They're all over me," Sam said, "and sooo itchy!"

"You need to see a doctor—what did Nurse Harrigan say?"

"She doesn't know."

"Why not? Come on, you have to see her."

But Sam didn't move. "The Woodland Wildlifers—they're coming today, and if I don't . . . don't get to meet them then . . . then . . ." A tear rolled down Sam's face. His eyes looked desperate. "I was hoping they would be . . ." (big sob and a horrible snot-sniffing sound) ". . . my—my Forever Family and I could be happy like you."

"But you might be really sick." He certainly *looked* really sick. "They'll understand."

"No, no! You've forgotten what it's like. First impressions count! If I don't see them today they'll get nervous—and maybe get put off completely. I'm never going to find my Forever Family. I'm never going to be happy."

I'd known Sam my whole life. We'd been through some good times and some very bad times. And one thing I knew for sure was that he deserved to have the chance to be happy.

I had to help him.

"Give me a strand of your hair," I said.

"What—what for?"

"Just do it."

"This is crazy," Sam said, but he pulled out a strand of his hair—"Ouch!"—and gave it to me.

I found a bucket with some old rainwater in it, pulled the spell pendant off my neck, and emptied the appearance spell ingredients. Then I dropped Sam's strand of hair into the bucket and stirred it and the spell ingredients around and around clockwise with a twig.

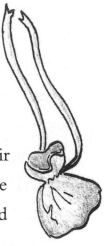

Sam was staring at me with his mouth open like I'd gone completely crazy.

"What are you doing?" he squeaked.

"Helping."

Sam's mouth was opening and closing like he didn't know what to say next.

I couldn't concentrate on pronouncing the difficult spell with him distracting me like that.

"Close your eyes."

"Why?"

"Just do it."

"I don't think I should."

"Now!"

Sam pretended to close his eyes but I'm pretty sure he was peeking.

I chanted the appearance spell three times and concentrated on thinking of a spot-free Sam, about his spots, fading, fading.

"Eeerooola eeeroolu mooozlar kal!"

I thought I'd said the words right. But would it work? I wanted it to work really, really badly. I wanted Sam to find a Forever Family and be just as happy as me.

And then it started. Sam's nasty rash was disappearing. The spell was working!

"It's stopped itching," he said.

But it didn't just stop where I wanted it to, maybe because I'd been concentrating so hard. Not only did Sam's rash fade away, but Sam was fading away, too! I started stirring counterclockwise, fast, and saying the spell backwards as Lilith had told us to do to reverse the spell.

"*Lak ralzooom ulooreee alooorreee.*"

But nothing happened. Sam was now invisible!

"Um, Sam . . . sorry . . . but . . ."

Sam opened his eyes. "What have you done? Where have my hands gone?" he screamed. "Where are my legs?"

"I'm sorry. I'm sorry. I didn't mean to . . ."

"Didn't mean to? Didn't mean to! You're only

supposed to *want* to be a witch—not go around
casting spells that work!"

"I didn't know it would. Not for sure."

"Make me visible again."

"I can't—I don't know how . . ."

"You made me *in*visible, you must be able to make me *visible*."

"I've already tried to reverse the spell—maybe I said it wrong. Maybe I shouldn't have said it so fast."

I tried saying the reversal spell again, only much slower, but Sam remained invisible.

"Why didn't you tell me you were a real . . . real witch?" he said.

"I'm just a witchling," I told him. "That's a trainee witch. I'm only just learning spells—I'm having lessons." And then I knew what I had to do.

I had to tell Lilith what I'd done and then I had to get her to tell me what to do. She was going to be very, very angry. But if I didn't tell her, then Sam might be stuck as the invisible boy forever.

"Wait here—I'll be back," I said.

Sam didn't want to wait. "No—what's going on?"

"Just wait here," I told him.

"What—or you'll turn me into a frog?"

"No, of course not. What do you think I am?"

Sam didn't say anything for a few seconds and then he gave a huge sigh. "The Woodland Wildlifers won't even be able to see me now. You've ruined everything."

"I'll fix it!"

I ran off towards my bike through the stinging nettles. I had to get back to Lilith quickly. I pedalled as fast as I could and finally I reached Coven Road.

"Lilith? Lilith, where are you?" I called, as I ran into the house.

But Lilith wasn't there. Where had she gone? I ran out into the garden.

"Lilith?" As I stood there, the flowers that only a second before had been blooming, started to shrivel. As I looked at my feet, the grass turned from green to brown.

I heard a crack and looked around to see one of the windows in our thatched cottage had broken. A second later another one broke. A chunk of thatch fell off the roof.

What was happening?

The Ice Palace bell started to ring.

Verity said it was only used for special occasions and emergencies. And this was no special occasion.

I felt scared. I had a nasty twisting feeling in my stomach. Something was very wrong. I ran out of the garden gate onto Coven Road. Our neighbors were running up the road toward the Ice Palace. Everywhere I looked, Coven Road, which had been so beautiful, was decaying and spoiling.

I shouted to Mrs. Turner, who had Waggy in her arms. "What's happening?"

"There's an uninvited non-witch in Coven Road!" she cried. "They managed to bypass the misdirection spell and the regular houses weren't in place."

There was suddenly a crack of thunder and it started to rain, even though it had been a clear day just moments before.

Zorellda would know what to do. I ran toward the Ice Palace with everyone else and squeezed into the back of the Great Hall. Most of the windows were cracked but the building was still standing. Every single one of the witches of Coven Road was gathered there, looking at the stage, waiting for the Grand Sorceress to tell them what to do.

Lilith saw me and pushed her way through and put her arm around me.

"Thank goodness you're all right," she said.

Zorellda raised her arms and the many voices quietened. "We must find the non-witch and banish whichever witch brought them here. Only then will this nightmare end."

"How do they know a witch brought them here?" I asked Lilith.

"There's only one way for a non-witch to bypass the misdirection spell and that's if a spell has been cast on them," she whispered back.

"What's going on?" a familiar voice behind me whispered.

I was about to reply when I realized who the voice belonged to. Sam! And he wasn't even invisible any more, not totally. He was a sort of shadowy outline.

Lilith was still looking at the stage.

"What are you doing here?" I hissed at Sam.

"Following you."

"I told you not to."

"And I did what you said—until I'd counted to ten and you were gone."

"You were supposed to wait until I got back," I whispered.

But Sam wasn't listening to me. "Lucky you're not all that fast on your bike or I'd have never seen where you went. This place is *seriously* weird. What's with all the houses falling down? This place is a health hazard. I bet Nurse Harrigan would be worried if she could see it."

I thought Nurse Harrigan would be even more worried if she found out I was living on a road full of witches. But I didn't tell Sam that.

I was just about to tell him to hide when I realized it was too late. Zorellda had seen him.

Lilith was staring at him and so was everyone else!

"I didn't. I didn't mean to . . ."

But as I said it, my heart sank and tears prickled my eyes as I realized that I'd broken all three of the promises I'd made—I'd used magic outside Coven Road, I'd told Sam that I was a witch, and I'd brought him to Coven Road. That would mean I would be banished.

Chapter 9

One second ticked past in silence . . . two seconds . . . three.

"*You* brought him here?" Zorellda said.

"Oh, Bella Donna," Lilith gasped. She looked so disappointed in me.

I'd let Lilith down badly. I'd let everyone down.

"It wasn't my fault!" I cried. "I told him to stay in the old greenhouse, but he followed me."

Sam, meanwhile, was becoming more and more visible—and so was his rash.

"The rest of you prepare the cauldron and bring whatever herbs and potions are still intact. Now we have the intruder and the culprit, at least the spell can be reversed," Zorellda said.

There was shuffling and pushing as everyone started to leave.

"Not you, Bella Donna," Zorellda said. "And not the non-witch."

All of the other witches, apart from Lilith, left. Most of them gave me nasty, accusing looks as they did so.

I felt very, very guilty. I hadn't meant to cause this much trouble. Not for one minute.

I felt something soft and furry brush past me.

Pegatha! I reached down to pick her up but she slipped past and went up onto the stage. She had something in her mouth. She dropped it in front of Zorellda. It looked like . . .

"That's my feather pen," Sam said.

"Is it indeed?" said Zorellda, raising an eyebrow.

"How did the cat get my pen?" Sam asked, looking confused. "I loaned it to Bella Donna."

"But I lost it," I said to him.

"I had it yesterday morning and then it disappeared, and I couldn't find it anywhere. I was going to tell you."

"You made a grave error of judgment by choosing to bring Bella Donna to Coven Road," Zorellda said to Lilith. "It was obviously too much for her. The temptation to break the rules was too great. I will see to this. You help the others with the cauldron."

Lilith pressed her lips together like she wanted to say something but knew she mustn't. She picked up Pegatha, who dropped the feather pen she'd been playing with, and left.

Through the window, the huge cauldron was clearly visible on the hill.

"You're not, um, you're not going to eat me, are you?" Sam said, sounding worried.

The logs beneath the cauldron were being lit. Sam swallowed hard.

"Eat you?" said Zorellda. "Of course we're not going to eat you—what a horrible thought. We're witches, not cannibals. Now come here so I can take a closer look at you."

Sam looked like he really, really didn't want to move, but he didn't have a choice—his legs started walking toward the stage. I followed close behind him. He wasn't invisible any more, but he still had the horrible multicolored rash.

"Who did this to you?" Zorellda asked him.

"Bella, but she was only trying to help. She was trying to take the rash away because my Forever Family might not like it, but instead of the rash fading away I faded away."

"But the rash is witch-made. Who gave you the rash?"

"I—I don't know. It just came . . ." Sam said, confused.

I was confused, too. What did Zorellda mean?

Zorellda looked thoughtful. "I see. Would you like me to make your skin problem disappear?"

"Yes," Sam said.

"And in return, do you promise you will never, ever reveal the secret of Coven Road or tell anyone about the witches that live here?"

"I promise," said Sam.

"Good," Zorellda said. She picked up Sam's pen and held it high above her head between her palms and said the reversal spell, "*Lak ralzooom ulooreee aloooreee.*"

Sam's nasty rash instantly disappeared and he was back to his old self.

"I could put a forgetting spell on you, but somehow I think I can trust you. And I've no doubt you would keep your promise because you've had a taste of the sort of things we're capable of," Zorellda said.

Sam was nodding his head very fast.

"Your Forever Family is waiting," Zorellda told him.

"B-Bye then," Sam said, and he started to back out of the Palace. "Bye, Bella."

"And Sam?" Zorellda added.

He stopped. "Yes?"

She almost smiled. "They were worth waiting for."

Sam turned and ran out of the Great Hall. I called after him that he could use my bike if he wanted to, but I don't think he heard me.

"I will deal with you once we've cast the illusion and misdirection spell and restored Coven Road," Zorellda said to me, though not unkindly. "Wait here."

She took Sam's feathery pen with her.

I waited and waited . . . and waited.

Zorellda seemed to be gone for a very long time. I watched the Ice Palace transform around me until it was back to its usual magnificent self but she still hadn't come back.

Then the door opened. But it wasn't Zorellda, it was Verity.

"Run!" she said.

"But Zorellda told me to—"

"All she's going to do when she comes back is banish you—if you run now then at least she won't be able to turn you into a frog, or something worse, as well as banishing you.

And Lilith wants you to leave, too—you let her down badly."

I felt like all my breath had been sucked out of me. I felt sick and my knees felt all wobbly. Lilith wanted me to leave. I wondered if I was going to faint, but I didn't.

"Look, you're my friend and I'm trying to help you, you idiot," said Verity. "Now run!"

And so I did.

I ran out of the Ice Palace—straight home to Lilith. Our thatched cottage was back to its usual self and the front door was open.

"Lilith, Lilith!" I called.

There was no answer. Lilith wasn't there. There was just Mystica, Bazeeta, Brimalkin, and Amelka staring down at me from the shelves.

I ran up to my room. Pegatha was on my bed.

I was going to miss her badly but I couldn't take her with me. I pulled out my suitcase, packed my clothes and my witch mobile, and left Coven Road.

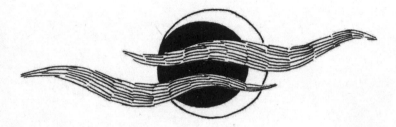

Chapter 10

I pedalled my bike all the way back to Templeton Children's Home again, which wasn't easy as I was carrying my suitcase at the same time. I was glad I was wearing my helmet as I nearly fell off my bike more than once. Trying to ride a bike while carrying a heavy suitcase and crying at the same time is definitely not a good idea.

As I got nearer, I realized I couldn't face Nurse Harrigan and her questions. "Did you say you wanted to be a witch?" she'd ask.

"Um . . ."

And then she'd be angry. "I told you not to say you wanted to be a witch, didn't I?"

I couldn't bear the thought of Maisie's pitying looks. She'd known how badly I'd wanted to be adopted by Lilith. My one and only chance and I'd messed it up. I'd used magic outside Coven Road when I'd promised, in front of everyone, that I wouldn't. I'd lost my Forever Family and I'd nearly ruined Sam's chance of having a Forever Family as well.

I hoped he was okay. I hoped the Woodland Wildlifers would turn out to be the Forever

Family he wanted. I hoped he'd be happy. One of us deserved to be.

The disappointment in Lilith's eyes—knowing she thought I'd let her down—had been too much to stand.

As I cycled through the gates of Templeton it started to rain. Just my luck. Now I was outside the children's home but I didn't want to go inside and face the music. I thought of the old greenhouse; no one besides Sam would think to look for me there and hopefully he'd be too busy meeting the Woodland Wildlifers to look.

Once I'd gotten past the stinging nettles and was inside the greenhouse I had a long cry. The thing I'd wanted to be more than anything in the world—a witch—had lost me my Forever Family. I wished I'd never wanted to be one. I wished I'd never gone to Coven Road. I wished I'd never learned the appearance spell.

I was wishing I had a tissue when I realized a very large worm was crawling over my foot—yuck.

Luckily it slid off and went on its way. The worm made me think of Sam's pen and that made me think of Pegatha. Why had she brought Sam's pen to Zorellda?

Could she have found it in my room? Was that where I'd lost it? But I'd looked everywhere for it once I'd realized it was missing. I knew how much Sam loved that pen. It didn't make sense.

I thought about the mistake I'd made using magic outside Coven Road. I'd promised not to use it except in cases of dire emergency—but to me, Sam's case had been a dire emergency. As I thought about the spots, I suddenly remembered what Zorellda had said—that the rash was witch-made. Who could possibly want to give Sam a rash? Unless . . . Lilith said that to make the appearance spell work on someone else you had to have something of theirs—a strand of hair or a piece of jewelry—or . . . or . . . a pen! And Zorellda had used Sam's pen to reverse the rash spell . . .

Then I remembered how Verity had volunteered to clean the cauldron after our last lesson and how long she'd taken doing it. Sam's pen had been on the table. She'd have had plenty of time to cast her own spell. Or maybe she'd taken the pen with her and cast the spell later when she was at home—her mom was always out so Verity could do what she liked. The more I thought about it, the more sure I was that Verity had done it. Verity had put the nasty rash spell on Sam!

But what I didn't know was *why* she'd done it . . .

I heard a sound outside and crouched down because I didn't want anyone to see me. I peeped out through the green sludged glass.

It was Sam. He'd got himself even muddier than usual. He'd really need to smarten himself up if he—

Two very muddy-looking people, even muddier than Sam and wearing wellington boots, came up behind him.

"There are lots of frogs over this way," Sam told them. He sounded happy and excited.

They didn't stop at the greenhouse and they didn't see me. I sat down on an empty tub that was a bit too small to sit on and then almost fell off it when I heard a meow.

Pegatha came into the greenhouse, rubbed herself against my legs, and purred.

"Oh Pegatha!" I buried my face in her soft fur. "Did you follow me?" I was very pleased to see her but she made me want to start crying all over again.

Then I saw that Lilith was right behind Pegatha.

"Lilith! What are you doing here?" I said.

"Oh, Bella, I've been looking for you everywhere! Pegatha led me here. Why did you run away?" She looked really worried.

I explained how sorry I was that I had broken all the rules and that I knew she didn't want me to live with her any more.

Lilith was very quiet as she listened, and then she said, "Whatever made you think that? Whatever you've done or do, you're my daughter and we stick together through thick and thin."

"We do?"

"We do."

"That's just what a Forever Family should be like," I said, feeling a little tearful, but in a happy way.

Pegatha purred.

"But Verity said . . . told me . . ." and then I paused. I suddenly remembered that I thought Verity had put a spell on Sam.

"Poor Verity," Lilith said. "She admitted everything to Zorellda. She's always been a jealous sort of girl and I suppose when you moved in and she saw you being so happy—well, she just had to spoil it. She was upset that it was no longer just her and me doing spell lessons. You were—are—very talented at casting spells and it was difficult for her to see you doing so well. She was used to being the only child in Coven Road and while it was nice for her to have company, it must have been hard for her when you came. She knew that you would do everything you could to help Sam. She wanted you to cast a spell outside Coven Road, and she intended to tell everyone what you had done so that you would be banished. Her plan went better than she'd ever imagined—Sam actually followed you to Coven Road. As you have seen, a non-witch on Coven Road can result in dire consequences. Still, we can only feel sorry for her."

I wasn't feeling quite so sorry for her. "She nearly ruined everything for Sam," I said. She'd known about his Forever Family coming to meet him. Maybe she'd known that it would take a situation like that to get me to break my promise and help him.

Lilith sighed. "She has such problems."

"What will happen to her?" I asked.

Lilith didn't know how exactly, but she knew that Verity would be punished. "Zorellda will see to all that. I don't think she'll banish her because of her age, but at the very least she'll be banned from using magic for a very, very long time."

Now that would be hard. I'd hate not being able to learn magic. I'd loved our spell classes. I loved being a witchling . . .

"Does that mean I can still be a witchling and we can still live on Coven Road?" I asked.

"Yes, of course."

I didn't want to cry any more. My grin was so huge it was much bigger than a Cheshire cat's. "I want to go home," I said. "I want to live with you and Pegatha and I want to learn how to be a witchling and then one day I want to be a witch, just like you."

Sam tapped on the greenhouse glass, waved, and came in.

"Hello, you three," he said, as if he was always finding Lilith and me and Pegatha in the old greenhouse, as if every day he went to Coven Road and met witches, got a nasty rash, and was turned invisible and back to visible again. "Meet Trevor and Tracy," he said, and the Woodland Wildlifers came into the greenhouse, too. "We're building a worm house for Templeton. And then . . ." Sam's grin got even bigger. "I'm going to their house and if we all get along okay—"

"Which I'm sure we will," said Trevor.

"Sam's just our kind of person," Tracy added.

Sam smiled up at Trevor and Tracy and they smiled back at him. He looked like he'd been with them forever—just the way a Forever Family should look.

". . . then I'll have a trial adoption and if that works out . . ."

"They'll be your Forever Family," I finished.

"What are you all doing in here?" Nurse Harrigan said, carefully avoiding the stinging nettles, which was just about impossible to do as there were so many of them. It was getting very crowded.

"We're saying hello to Sam's new family," said Lilith.

"Oh, that's kind. Isabella and he have been through a lot together," Nurse Harrigan said.

I looked at Sam and Sam looked at me—we had been through a lot, especially that day!

"Let's get that worm house finished," said Trevor.

"See you at school tomorrow, Bella," said Sam.

Regular school was going to feel very ordinary after all this. But I was looking forward to seeing Angela and Rajni and Ellen, even though I couldn't tell them about any of what had happened or that I was a witchling. They probably wouldn't have believed me anyway.

I picked up Pegatha. It was time to go home to Coven Road.

Join Bella Donna online!

Be a part of Coven Road and
keep up to date with the latest
Bella Donna news.

Find out more about Coven Road,
the characters, and much more!

BellaDonnaOnline.co.uk

Bella Donna

Too Many Spells

Half the time Bella Donna is a regular girl at a regular school with her regular friends—animal-mad Sam and pink-fan Angela. The other half of the time she's a young witch working very hard at learning her spells, and she is desperate to win the Spell Casting Contest.

But a new teacher at school is making her nervous. Witchlike things are happening in the classroom, and Bella knows it isn't her doing them . . .

Coming soon.